HELLO? IS ANYBODY THERE?

BY THE SAME AUTHOR
The Christmas Mystery
The Solitaire Mystery
Sophie's World
That Same Flower

HELLO? IS ANYBODY THERE?

JOSTEIN GAARDER

TRANSLATED BY JAMES ANDERSON

ILLUSTRATED BY SALLY GARDNER

FARRAR, STRAUS AND GIROUX • NEW YORK

Farrar, Straus and Giroux
19 Union Square West, New York 10003

Copyright © 1996 by Gyldendal Norsk Forlag
Translation copyright © 1997 by James Anderson
Translation revisions copyright © 1997
by Orion Children's Books
Illustrations copyright © 1997 by Sally Gardner
All rights reserved
Distributed in Canada by Douglas & McIntyre Ltd.
Printed in the United States of America
First published in 1996 by Gyldendal Norsk Forlag as
Hallo? Er det noen her?
First Farrar, Straus and Giroux edition, 1998

Library of Congress Cataloging-in-Publication Data
Gaarder, Jostein.
　[Hallo? Er det noen her?　English]
　Hello? Is anybody there? / Jostein Gaarder ; translated
by James Anderson ; illustrated by Sally Gardner.
　　p.　　cm.
　Summary: While waiting for the birth of his baby
brother, Joe is visited by a strange child from another
planet, and the two discover that they, and their plan-
ets, share many similarities as well as differences.
　ISBN 0-374-32948-6
　[1. Extraterrestrial beings—Fiction.]　I. Anderson,
James.　II. Gardner, Sally, ill.　III. Title.
PZ7.G1114Hg　1998
[Fic]—dc21　　　　　　　　　　　　*98-23916*
　　　　　　　　　　　　　　　　　　　　AC

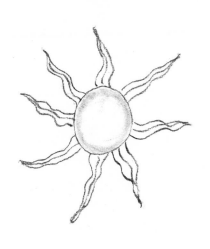

THE SKY

Dear Camilla,

When you were spending your vacation here, I promised to write you a story. Well, here it is.

I'm sitting down to write to you today for a special reason. It's nearly your birthday, and you are going to be exactly the same age as I was when I was waiting for my baby brother to be born. So I thought I should tell you about Mika. Then you'll understand it all.

Do you remember all the things we did together when you were here? Do you remember how we caught crabs in the little cove where I keep my boat? And how we used to look at the stars every night through my big telescope, and how we made pancakes on the one night it was cloudy? I often think about that week and what a good time we had.

I can remember lots of things about Mika,

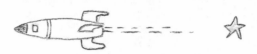

too. I don't pretend to recall everything as if it happened yesterday—it's more like last week! I'm sure I've forgotten some bits and imagined others, but it's often like that when we try to describe things that happened a long time ago.

I remember clearly enough how it all started. You might say it began quite normally—if you can call waiting for a little sister or brother normal, that is. I'm not so sure you can. Things aren't always as ordinary as we may think.

In those days we kept a couple of hens scratching about in the garden. Do you think a hen is ordinary? Well, I did too. But that was before I met Mika.

Imagine you were a lone spaceman crisscrossing back and forth through outer space.

Even if you traveled for an eternity, you'd be lucky to see a single hen.

There are billions and billions of stars in the vast expanse of outer space we call the universe. A few of these stars have a planet or two moving around and around them on a set path called an orbit. After traveling for hundreds, if not thousands, of years, you might possibly get to a planet with life on it. But even if there were living things there, the chances of finding a hen are extremely slim. You might find an egg, but I doubt that a chicken would hatch out of it.

There are probably no hens anywhere else in the universe except on our own earth. And the universe is unimaginably vast! So we can hardly call a hen ordinary!

While we're on the subject of hens, did you know that it is possible for a hen to lay a new egg almost every day? Have you heard of any other bird or animal that does that?

The reason I'm beginning my story like this is that Mika was the one who taught me that nothing is ordinary. Sometimes people talk about "an ordinary day." This annoys me, because no two days are the same, and we have no idea how many more days of life we have left. Perhaps even worse than "ordinary" hens or "ordinary" days is talking about an "ordinary" boy or girl. This is the sort of thing we say when we can't be bothered to get to know people better.

So there I was, waiting for a little sister or brother. My family were always discussing which it would be. Personally, I felt sure that the big lump in Mom's tummy was a boy. I don't know why I was so sure—perhaps it was just that I wanted a brother more than anything else.

We humans like to believe in the things we want most. It was hard to imagine what it would be like to have a baby brother, but I knew he would be at least a bit like me. A sister was much harder to picture.

Mom said the baby was lying upside down inside her and kicking her tummy black-and-blue. When I heard this, I thought my baby brother ought to pull himself together. That was the first time I felt like giving him a word of advice—it certainly wasn't the last. But we are born into this world without any manners at all. It takes years for us to learn to show a little consideration for others.

I knew my baby brother would find it strange arriving in a totally new world. I didn't envy him. When he did come he'd have to get used to lots of different things. He couldn't have much idea of what it was like outside the small dark space in which he found himself.

I had already begun to think carefully about how I would explain it all to him. I would have to tell him what everything in the world was like.

My baby brother had never been in the world before. He had never seen the sun and the stars, the flowers and animals in the fields, and he wouldn't know what they were all called. I had a good deal more to learn myself. For instance, I didn't know the difference between a jaguar and a leopard. I now know that they both have spots, but their spots are

arranged in different patterns. But that's not the point. There are thousands of different animals on this planet. For a long time to come I would have my hands full teaching my baby brother the difference between a dog and a cat.

It's taken human beings thousands of years
to name all the plants and animals in creation,
and we still haven't finished. So one lifetime
seems rather a short span in which to learn
them all.

My baby brother was just like an astronaut visiting earth for the very first time.

"Hello? Is anybody there? Or is it all empty and deserted? A blue planet! It looks like a jawbreaker. Could there be life on it? Help! I'm falling!"

I was only eight when all this happened. It began at night. I was dreaming . . .

"Wake up, Joe," said Dad. "The baby's on the way!"

"But it's the middle of the night!" I said, sitting right up in bed. "He's not supposed to arrive yet. Auntie Helen's not here!"

"Babies do sometimes decide to arrive early," said Dad. "They don't know what day or time it is. I'll have to drive Mom to the hospital. I've phoned Auntie Helen, and she's coming as quickly as she can, but I'm afraid you'll have to wait here on your own till she gets here."

15

Mom and Dad had arranged for Auntie Helen to come and look after me when the baby was born, but she wasn't due for another week.

That wouldn't happen now, Camilla—your mother would take you to the hospital with her. But when I was your age, children often went around on their own or stayed at home when their parents went out. I didn't mind. I was used to being in the house alone.

I said I'd be all right until Auntie Helen arrived. "I'll build something with my Lego," I said.

I had built some huge space rockets. I really had to use my imagination, because you couldn't buy any special Lego spaceship kits in those days.

I got dressed
quickly. I was
looking forward to
the birth of my
little brother.
This'll put an end
to all his kicking, I
thought. And it had
been weeks since I'd
last sat on Mom's lap.

I remember going to the window and
releasing the blind. It rolled up with a snap,
then whirled around and around. I peered up
into the star-spangled heavens. It was the
clearest night sky I'd ever seen.

I ran downstairs. Mom was sitting in an
armchair clutching her back. Her eyes were
closed tight, and all the muscles in her face
were tense.

Dad had told me that giving birth was
always hard work, so I didn't want to disturb
her. I felt like saying that getting a baby sister or
brother could be rather hard, too, but that
would have to wait for another time.

It was still pitch-black when Mom and Dad
drove off and the car's lights disappeared.

I knew they weren't thinking about me at

all. That was the worst thing. The tiny baby that had begun to fight its way out of Mom's tummy was more than enough to occupy them.

For a long time I stood in the doorway. When I went back in again, closing the front door behind me, the house felt as deserted as outer space.

2

THE
GARDEN

I remember going back up to my room and sitting on a chair in front of the window. There I stayed for a long time, gazing up at the stars. I was wondering if there were any planets with life on them out there, or if our earth was the only one in the entire universe. I was alone in the house, and it was a little boring, being on my own.

As I sat there, it began to get lighter outside. The sky had turned from inky black to dark blue. Because the house was so still, I could hear the waves lapping against the dock where we kept our boat, down in the cove.

I wasn't really afraid of the dark. I was used to thinking about outer space, because I was always building spaceships and lunar modules. But just then something happened that made me jump.

Suddenly a shooting star streaked across the sky, so close that it looked as if it were going to land in the garden right in front of me.

I had heard that a shooting star crosses the sky each time someone is born. Maybe that shooting star was for my baby brother.

Exactly what happened next I'm not sure, but all at once I heard a commotion in the garden. For a second I thought it must be Mom and Dad back from the hospital with the baby. I leaned out the window and spied a small boy dangling from the apple tree. It was Mika.

It was only much later that I realized how lucky he had been. Not only had he fallen into the apple tree, but his pants had got hitched up in it and had left him hanging upside down in mid-air. If he'd come down in Mom's rose bed, he would have hurt himself badly.

I tore down the stairs, charged into the garden, and raced toward the boy in the tree.

"It must be a dream!" said the boy.

Those were the very first words he spoke. I thought they were rather odd, because I was wide-awake.

This boy didn't look like you or me, Camilla. His eyes and mouth and ears showed quite clearly that he didn't come from around here. But I didn't know he had fallen out of a spaceship! I wasn't really surprised that he could speak English. When a real live boy falls out of the sky, it doesn't much matter what language he speaks. It was amazing that he could speak at all.

"It must be a dream," repeated the boy.

By now all sorts of things were chasing through my head at once. Who was this boy in the tree? And if this was a dream, would it be his dream—or mine? And if it was his dream, how could I be wide-awake?

What would you say if you had a visit from outer space?

He was still dangling in the tree, spinning slowly around and around. My head was spinning, too.

I didn't know what to say, but I remembered something I'd been thinking as I sat up in my room looking at the stars. I'd been thinking how dull it was on my own. The next moment, here was a small boy hanging in the apple tree. Not all wishes are granted that quickly.

"Who are you?" he asked.

"My name's Joe," I said.

"And I'm Mika. Why are you standing upside down?"

I couldn't help laughing. He suddenly stuck a thumb into his mouth and began to suck it like a baby. Maybe he was embarrassed.

"You're the one who's upside down," I said.

Mika pulled the thumb out of his mouth, and all his fingers began to wave.

"When two people meet," he said, "and one is upside down, it isn't always easy to tell which of them is the right way up."

I was so taken aback by this that I could think of nothing to say.

Mika pointed to the ground.

"All the same, it would be nice if you could help me up to this planet's surface."

"Down!" I said.

"No, up!" said Mika.

I ran to the shed and fetched the heavy shears Mom used for tending the roses. There was an old milk crate there, so I placed it under the tree and stood on it. Then I cut Mika down from the branch.

He stayed still for a while. I can remember being very impressed with the way he could stand on his head without using his hands.

His eyes rolled around and around and darted from side to side. I suppose he was trying to take in his surroundings. Then he caught sight of the sky above him. Only then did he lower his legs to the ground. He stayed on his knees for a little while, then got to his feet and looked about him in bewilderment.

"Where have you come from?" I ventured to ask.

"I was in a spaceship," said Mika. "I saw I was near a planet with living things on it, so I opened the hatch to have a look, and I fell out."

He pointed down at the grass.

"I thought that was up," he said.

Then he pointed up at the sky.

"And I thought that was down."

He waved his fingers around again.

"I know I was traveling upward from my planet, until I banged my head on your planet," he said.

Finally, he pointed at the moon.

"I noticed this planet had a moon," he said. "When you go there, do you travel upward or downward?"

"Upward," I said.

The first man had landed on the moon only a few weeks before, so I knew what I was talking about.

Mika had put his thumb in his mouth again. He took it out because he had another question.

"But when you land on the moon, don't you fly down to the moon's surface?"

I had to think carefully. I nodded. "Yes."

"And when you're there, don't you look up at this planet?"

I'd never been to the moon myself, but I'd watched all the moon-landing programs on television. I nodded again.

What is up and what is down?   27

"So somewhere between this planet and the moon, down becomes up and up becomes down?"

I thought about this. It sounded right.

"Yes, I suppose they must," I admitted.

"I think I know the exact spot where the change takes place," said Mika thoughtfully.

Suddenly he began to bound about the garden like a kangaroo. First he tried some light, wary hops, then he jumped as high as he could.

"Your planet can't be as big as mine," he said. "Its gravity isn't as strong, at any rate."

I looked at him, puzzled.

"Don't you know what gravity is?" Mika went on. "It's an invisible force that pulls you and everything else toward the planet's surface, no matter where you are. If there was no gravity at all, everything would fall off the planet and hurtle into space. On your planet, I can jump twice as high as I can on my own, because the gravity here is weaker. If you were to come home with me, you might not be able to jump at all."

It seemed unfair that he could jump higher than I could, just because he came from a planet with more gravity. But it gave me something to think about. I remembered the men I had watched jumping on the moon. They jumped much farther than we could, even wearing their bulky space suits. That must mean that the gravity on the moon is even less than the gravity on the earth, and a lot less than the gravity on Mika's planet.

As soon as Mika had finished testing gravity, he got down on all fours and examined the grass. He smelled it, then pulled up a few green tufts and put them in his mouth. He spat them out in a hurry.

"You shouldn't eat grass. It doesn't taste nice," I said.

He spluttered several times and spat again. I felt a little sorry for him. If he'd come all the way from another planet, he must be hungry. So I ran to the apple tree and picked up an apple from the ground. I thought I ought to try to be a bit welcoming on behalf of the planet I lived on.

"Try an apple," I said, offering him the green fruit.

I could tell he was looking at an apple for

the very first time. At first he just sniffed it, then he ventured to take a small bite.

"Yum-yum," he said. He took a bigger bite.

"Do you like it?" I asked.

He made a deep bow.

"What did it taste like?" I asked. I wanted to know what it's like to eat your very first apple.

He bowed and bowed.

"Why are you bowing?" I asked.

"Where I come from, we always bow when someone asks an interesting question," Mika explained. "And the deeper the question, the deeper we bow."

This was one of the silliest things I'd ever heard. I couldn't see how a question was anything to bow about.

"So what do you do when you greet each other, then?" I asked.

"We try to think of a clever question," he replied.

"Why?"

I'd asked another question, so he gave a quick bow. Then he said:

"We try to find something clever to ask so the other person has to bow."

This answer impressed me so much that I gave the deepest bow I could. When I looked up again, Mika was sucking his thumb. There was a long pause before he took it out.

"Why did you bow?" he asked, sounding rather offended.

"Because you gave such a clever answer to my question," I replied.

"But an answer is never worth bowing for," said Mika. "Even if it sounds clever and correct, you still shouldn't bow for it."

I nodded, but I was sorry the moment I'd done it, in case Mika thought I was bowing for the answer he'd just given.

"When you bow, you give way," continued Mika. "You must never give way to an answer."

"Why not?"

"An answer is always the stretch of road that's behind you. Only a question can point the way forward."

His words sounded so wise that I had to stop myself from bowing again.

Just then the sun rose on a new day. Mika tugged at my sweater and pointed up at the red rim.

"What's the name of that star?" he asked.

"That's the sun," I answered.

Mika began to stretch and splay out his fingers.

"But it's still a star," he said. "Every sun is a star, and all stars are suns. It's just that not all stars have planets orbiting them, and, in any case, if a planet doesn't have living beings on it to look at its star, there's no one around to call that star the sun."

I realized Mika was right. I wanted to say something clever too.

"It must be lonely being a star with no planets to shine on," I said, "because if a star hasn't got any planets to shine on, no one can look up at it when it rises on a new day."

"You can look up at it," said Mika.

"Me?"

"Yes. You can look at the lonely star when it rises on a new night. The darker the night, the more suns we can see in the sky. During the day we can only see our own."

This was what my first meeting with Mika was like. He sucked his thumb when he was deep in thought and fanned his fingers out when he wanted to explain something.

Whenever I asked a good question, he bowed low. And when I answered, he would listen carefully to see if he could ask me another question.

I didn't realize he could turn sulky until after a telephone call . . .

3

THE
HOUSE

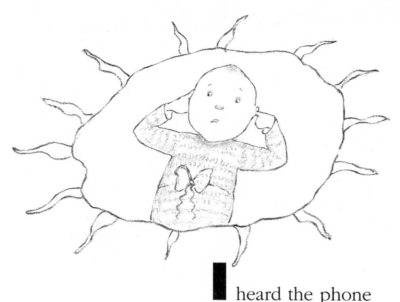

I heard the phone start ringing indoors. Mika did too. He suddenly began shaking his head and trying to clear his ears.

"There's a horrid sound in my ears," he exclaimed in panic.

This made me laugh. "It's just a telephone," I told him.

But that made him even more frightened.

"Is it dangerous getting a telephone in your ear?" he asked.

"It isn't in your ear," I explained. I hadn't time to tell him any more because I had to hurry back to the house to answer it. Mika trotted along behind me.

It was Dad.

"Hello, Joe. We're at the hospital. Everything's okay, but the baby's not going to

be here for another few hours. Are you all right?
Has Auntie Helen arrived?"

"She's not here yet, but don't worry, I'm
fine," I said.

Just then Mika stormed out of the hallway
and into the kitchen. He stood on a chair and
clambered right up onto the counter.

"I wonder why Auntie Helen's taking such a
long time," said Dad. He sounded anxious.

Mika had reached up and pulled one of the
cupboard doors open.

"Are you sure you're all right, Joe?" said Dad.

Just then a large bag of flour toppled out of the cupboard.

"Oh yes, quite sure," I said.

I was watching Mika try to create a snowstorm in the kitchen, but I couldn't say anything to Dad. I couldn't tell him I had a visitor from outer space.

"What are you up to, then?" he asked.

At that moment Mika started to sneeze. He was sneezing and laughing in turns.

"Nothing," I said. "I've got to go. Bye, Dad!"

I rushed over, put my arms around Mika, and lifted him down to the floor.

"What are you doing?" I said.

Mika just looked up at me and laughed, so I said sternly, "You mustn't touch things!"

At this Mika began to bawl. He made so much noise that I had to stick my fingers in my ears. It didn't look as if he was likely to calm down for a long time, and I could hardly go around with my fingers in my ears until Auntie Helen arrived. I had to try to think of something that would make him stop.

First I waved my hands about and made funny faces. When that didn't work, I began to dance around the kitchen floor. I tried balancing on one leg and crowing like a cock, then hopping to and fro in front of him. Nothing helped, so finally I took a handful of flour from the bag and tossed it into the air. I thought Mika might be sulking because he hadn't been allowed to play with the flour. But still he wouldn't stop. He only yelled louder and louder, and every new piece of clowning I tried just made me feel sillier.

Then I had a brilliant idea. I sat down beside him and began to tickle his neck with my finger. His crying eased off right away, then ceased altogether. At that point I stopped my tickling, but it was a mistake because he began crying again. So I quickly went on tickling him and stroked his cheek as well. I noticed that his skin felt different from yours or mine.

At last all was quiet in the kitchen, but I went on stroking Mika's cheek for a long while.

From time to time I took a little rest and said some soothing words. Gradually, I made these breaks longer until I dared to take my hands away completely.

After that I thought I'd better clean up the mess in the kitchen. I managed to sweep up most of the flour that had spilled on the floor, and tipped it into the sink. Then I sat down beside Mika again.

"On this planet you're not allowed to waste food," I said.

I tried to say it in a kind and friendly way so he wouldn't start crying again, but he was still a bit sulky.

"It's just a dream, so anything's allowed," he said crossly.

I didn't like this talk about everything being just a dream.

"You can't be dreaming about me," I said. "I'm wide-awake. And besides, I really live here."

I remember his exact reply.

"But I don't. So I must be dreaming."

I couldn't piece any of this together properly. I was even more confused when he said:

"I must hurry back before I start waking up.

If I don't, I'll never find my way home."

He didn't get the chance to say any more, because at that moment the doorbell rang.

Mika shook his head and began trying to clear his ears again.

"It's the telephone!" he exclaimed.

"It's Auntie Helen," I shouted.

What was I to do now? I couldn't just let Auntie Helen in and tell her I had a visitor from outer space. I'd have to try and hide Mika.

I knew lots of fantastic hiding places in the house, but this time it wasn't just an object I was trying to conceal. I had to hide a living boy who would start howling the moment he was upset. I couldn't even say that Mika was a friend who'd come to visit. I've told you, Camilla, he didn't look exactly like you or me.

The doorbell rang again. I knew we'd have to move fast.

"Shall we play hide-and-seek?" I asked.

He seemed to know what I meant by this. If there was life on other planets, there were bound to be good hiding places, too. And wherever there were lots of hiding places, someone must have discovered they could play hide-and-seek. I believe I can remember thinking that one of the first things people would learn on any planet was how to play hide-and-seek.

I took Mika's hand and led him up to my room. As we went up the stairs he peered about the house in amazement.

"You can hide in my room," I said. "But you mustn't make a sound."

The doorbell rang for the third time. I ran down to the hall and opened the door.

Auntie Helen looked as startled as if she'd tumbled off the moon, though she wasn't the one I'd cut loose from the apple tree in the garden. For a second I wondered if Mika was standing in the hallway behind me.

"Oh, Joe, I'm sorry I'm so late. I should have been here hours ago! The car broke down. Are you all right? Why are you looking such a mess?" she asked. "And why didn't you open the door when I rang?"

She wasn't cross. But she had asked three questions. I bowed three times.

"What are you bowing for?" she demanded.

I bowed again and said:

"In this house we always bow low when someone asks an interesting question."

Auntie Helen pushed past me through the hall and into the kitchen. When she saw it, she asked another question.

"Joe, really! What have you been up to?"

The flour! I didn't know what to say. Then I remembered something that had come to me while I'd been sweeping up.

"I was going to make pancakes," I said. In my family we always had pancakes on special occasions.

She bent down and gave me a hug. "Just think, you're going to have a little sister or brother," she said.

"Brother," I said.

Auntie took me into the bathroom and brushed off all the flour that covered my

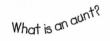

What is an aunt?

clothes. She promised she'd make pancakes for lunch. So, in a way, I had Mika to thank for that.

I still hadn't had any breakfast, but I was so scared that Auntie Helen would go up to my room while I sat eating in the kitchen that I didn't mention it. As soon as she'd sat down in the big wing chair in the living room, I was up the stairs.

"I'm going to build something with my Lego," I said.

Mika had made no attempt to hide. He was sitting on the bed staring at my big dinosaur book. He hardly even bothered to look up when I came in. He had my magnifying glass in one hand.

"Are there lots of animals like this around here?" he asked.

"Ssh!" I whispered.

I clambered up onto the bed beside him.

"Those are dinosaurs," I said. "They were huge animals that lived here millions of years ago, but they all died out."

Mika opened his eyes wide.

"Before they could develop?"

I nodded.

"Before they could turn into human beings?"

Even in those days I knew something about the history of the planet, but this question seemed so odd that I didn't know how to answer.

"There weren't any human beings living here then," I explained.

"So where do you come from?" asked Mika.

I forgot to bow for his question. Perhaps that was why he didn't wait for an answer. He started pointing at all the letters in the book.

"And what are all these little pictures? They're so tiny they hurt my eyes."

"Ssh! They're letters," I whispered. I hadn't forgotten Auntie Helen sitting downstairs in the living room imagining I was playing with my Lego.

a b c d e f g h i

j k l m n o p q r

s t u v w x y z

"But what are they *for*?"

It isn't easy to explain what letters are to someone who can't read.

"Well, there are twenty-six different letters," I began.

"They're not all different. Some of them are exactly the same," said Mika. "Anyway, they're drawings, aren't they?"

"We call them letters," I said. "We put them together to make up words, and when we look at them it's called reading."

Mika looked puzzled.

"The words in this book," I continued, "are all about dinosaurs."

Mika pushed the book with all its letters close up to his face so that he could see them better. He tried to hold the big magnifying glass in between. Then he let the book drop back into his lap.

"It's no good!" he said. "I can't tell what they mean."

"Shall I read to you?" I asked.

He pushed the book into my lap, and I started to read the beginning of the story of the dinosaurs, following the words with my finger as I read.

"Dinosaurs were the biggest land animals that have ever lived, but no human being has seen any live ones, because the last dinosaurs died out sixty-five million years ago, way, way before humans existed. Scientists have

discovered what shape they were and that they hatched from eggs, because they have found fossils of their bones, teeth, droppings, and eggs buried in rocks. After the dinosaurs died out, mammals became the most important—"

"What are mammals?" Mika interrupted.

"Animals that give birth to live babies are mammals," I explained. "Like cats and cows and elephants and whales."

"But all babies are alive," Mika interrupted again.

I was about to explain that another difference between mammals and other animals is that the young are fed on their mother's milk when I heard Auntie Helen's voice.

"Joe! Don't you want some breakfast?" she called.

"No thanks!" I called back, though it wasn't really true.

Then I heard her making her way upstairs.

"I'm coming!" I shouted.

I rushed out onto the landing and bumped into Auntie Helen on the stairs. "Oops!"

50

She stopped. "What's the matter, Joe?"

"Nothing! Just going out to play."

If Auntie had taken it into her head to look into my room, she would have had the shock of her life. Fortunately, she was so flustered that she turned on the stairs and followed me down instead.

I had to think of something to say before I reached the front door, so that I'd have a chance of smuggling Mika out of the house. Just then I noticed the vacuum cleaner in the living room.

"Are you going to do some cleaning?" I asked.

She nodded. "There's flour absolutely every-where."

"Sorry, Auntie Helen!" I said. "Well, I sup-pose I'd better not hold you up!"

She shook her head despairingly, then plugged in the vacuum cleaner and switched it on.

At that, I ran up to my room again.

Mika was petrified. He was sitting on the bed with his hands clamped over his ears.

"It's only a vacuum cleaner," I told him. "It'll clean up the mess. Now we can sneak out."

I took his hand and led him down the

stairs. It felt nice to have a small hand nestling in mine.

By the time we got down to the hall, Auntie Helen had gone into the kitchen.

Fortunately, she was standing with her back to us. Mika glanced at her before we made for the door. I don't think he had the slightest wish to be introduced.

Once in the garden he did some more kangaroo hops. He cavorted and yodeled as if he'd been sleeping for a hundred years and had only just woken up.

I had one thing on my mind. The house had lots of windows overlooking the garden, so we couldn't stay here. But I had a plan . . .

THE SEA

I ran to the currant bushes at the bottom of the garden, where the path leading down to the sea began. Looking back, I saw Mika running in zigzags and turning somersaults. At least he was following me.

Then he stretched up and smelled one of the currant bushes. He had the magnifying glass with him. He lifted it to his face and chortled to see how big it made the red berries.

As soon as we were hidden by the currant bushes, I turned to him.

"Can you hear anything?" I asked.

He stood listening for a few moments.

"Someone's splashing water," he replied.

"That's the sea," I said proudly. "The sea splashes by itself."

We got down to the large smooth rock that lay on a slope above the little cove where we

kept our boat. I was allowed this far on my
own, and not a step farther. I sat down on a
shelf in the rock, the one Mom sometimes
called the Stone Seat. Mika sat down beside me.

The sun was already high
in the sky. It glittered and
sparkled so brightly on
the water that Mika
had to squint. Perhaps
he isn't used to such
strong sunlight, I
thought.

All of a sudden he lifted the magnifying
glass toward the sun so that he could examine it
more closely. I managed to save him just in
time.

"Be careful!" I exclaimed. "You must never
do that!"

At that he began to scream again. I was
terrified Auntie Helen would hear him from the
house. But now I knew what to do. I placed my
fingers in the nape of his neck and started
stroking and tickling him.

"There, there," I said.

It worked almost immediately.

I remembered that Dad and I had once lit a
fire just by holding the lens from an old tele-

scope over wood. I explained to
Mika that the magnifying glass
would bring the sun's rays
together to a sharp point. I
told him it was even possible
to set fire to a piece of paper
with a magnifying glass.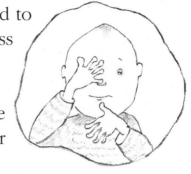

He was still crying gently, but I think that
was just so that I'd keep tickling his neck.

"Tell me about the sea," he said, as I
stroked him. "Are there any animals in it?"

"Lots," I replied.

"But no dinosaurs?"

I shook my head. Then I began telling Mika
about the sea.

I loved finding out about science and
natural history. I collected books about
dinosaurs, and I had learned a great deal about
the history of the earth from them too. I was
always talking to Dad about it. Now I told Mika
that all life on this planet came from the sea.

"Human beings too?" he asked.

I bowed deeply for this question. Then I
said: "People think that life on this planet began
three thousand million years ago. This means
that all the plants and animals on earth are
related to one another."

"But what about the dinosaurs?" said Mika.

"That's a long story," I said. And I began to tell him a little of the story.

"The very first animals lived in the sea. They were so small you couldn't even see them. For millions of years they were the only living things, but they kept on changing. Each of these changes was only tiny, but as time passed they made a big difference. A thousand million years is quite a help. That's a thousand times a thousand times a thousand.

"The first real animals that developed were jellyfish and flatworms, which had soft bodies and were big enough to pick up in your hands.

"After millions more years, animals with hard body coverings, such as shrimps and lobsters and crabs,

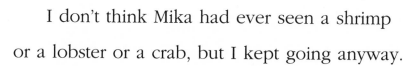

appeared in the sea."

I don't think Mika had ever seen a shrimp
or a lobster or a crab, but I kept going anyway.

"Another hundred million years or so later,
there were fish swarming about in
the oceans. Some of the fish developed into
amphibians—animals that could breathe both in
water and on dry land."

I knew I was using some difficult words,
but I had only just learned them and it was fun
to practice them.

"Are there any amphibians around now?"
asked Mika.

I could only think of frogs
and toads and salamanders,
but I said that many early forms of life still
existed on earth.

"But not dinosaurs?"
Mika persisted.

I shook my head. "Dinosaurs came much later, and there aren't any left."

"So what happened?" asked Mika.

"The amphibians came out of the sea to live in the swampy forests that began to spread over the earth. Millions of years went by, and some of the amphibians developed into reptiles. The dinosaurs were a kind of reptile. Even though there aren't any dinosaurs left, there are still lots of different reptiles, and some of them look a bit like dinosaurs."

Mika wasn't satisfied. He wanted to know more.

"And what sort of animal do you come from?"

"I'm a mammal, like all human beings," I explained. "Mammals developed from reptiles. The very first ones were small with big eyes and sharp brains, and they were covered with hair. There are hundreds of different sorts—bats, horses, lions, monkeys, wolves, and hippopotamuses. None of them lays eggs. They all give birth to live young."

We had talked about this before, but Mika had a puzzled look.

"Don't mammals need to lay an egg or two as well, before they can have live young?"

I found myself laughing again, because there was so much Mika didn't know about life on this planet. But in a way he was right. Female mammals do produce eggs, but the eggs don't need a hard shell. That's because an egg develops into a baby inside the mother's tummy. It grows and grows inside her, until it is fully formed and ready to come out into the world.

What is an egg?

I didn't even try to explain this last bit fully to Mika. The truth was that I didn't totally understand it myself.

Mika sat gazing out across the sea from which all life on this planet had once sprung.

"An egg is a miracle," he said at last.

That sounded very wise. But I still couldn't understand why he was so interested in eggs and dinosaurs.

All the time we'd been talking about the sea and how life on earth began, I'd been tickling Mika's neck. He obviously enjoyed it, for as soon as I stopped he jumped up and ran off down to the water. I wasn't allowed to do that. But I had no idea if Mika could swim and I couldn't risk letting him drown, so I leaped up from the Stone Seat and raced after him.

I thought back to something I'd been wondering while I was talking about the sea. As we'd neared the cove, Mika had heard the water splashing, so I knew he knew what it was.

"Is there any water on your planet?" I asked.

Mika bent down and thrashed his hands about in the sea. He ripped up a clump of sea-weed, waved it about in the air, and gave us both a cold shower.

"If there's life on any planet where there's

no water," he said, "it must be very different from life on your planet or mine."

Now that I had met someone who'd come all the way from another planet, I thought I'd better grab my chance and find out what I could. Mika knew so much more about outer space than I did! But then, he knew nothing about life on this planet. He had only been here a few hours.

"Do you think there's water on many planets?" I asked.

He bowed for the question, then shook his head.

"No. Planets with water mustn't be too close to the sun, for one thing, otherwise it would all dry up. But they can't be too far away, either, or the water would turn to ice."

Mika now ran onto the dock and clambered down into the rowboat. He jumped up and down in the boat, making it rock. I was terrified he'd fall overboard.

"Don't do that! You must never jump about in a boat!" I told him.

I was worried he'd start yelling and screaming because I'd told him not to do something. To avoid this, I came up with a clever idea.

"Would you like to learn how to row?" I

asked, even though I knew it was strictly forbid-
den.

I wasn't very good at rowing, but I showed
Mika how to use one oar, while I rowed with
the other. That was how Dad and I used to do
it. When we were well out into the cove, we
pulled in the oars and drifted.

There was a fishing line in the bottom of
the boat. It was Mika who bent down and
picked it up. Perhaps I should have warned him

not to, because he managed to prick himself on a fishhook that was tied to the line.

"Ouch!" he cried.

Luckily, the hook hadn't gone right in. But when I pulled it out of Mika's skin, I noticed a little drop of blood squeeze out from his finger. And that drop of blood wasn't red. It was dark blue—almost black.

That was because he came from another planet! Mika couldn't have developed from the fish in the sea, at least not from the fish in our seas, for fish have red blood, too. Maybe he wasn't even a mammal. But if he wasn't a mammal, what was he?

I didn't have time to think much about this because Mika immediately began to wail and make a fuss. I bent over him and tickled his neck.

"There, there!" I said, and he calmed down almost at once.

Since we'd had so much trouble with the fishhook, I thought I might as well explain what it was used for. Mika didn't need to be told twice. He cast out the line.

I'd often been out fishing with Dad. I'd had a few bites, but I'd only once landed a fish all on my own, so it didn't seem fair that Mika got a fish on his very first try.

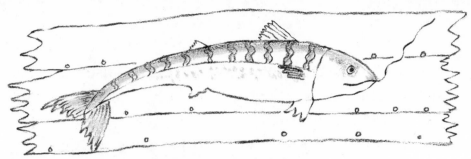

I saw the tugging on his line.

"You've got a bite!" I whispered.
"Now you must wind the line in."

Soon after, a mackerel lay floundering in the bottom of the boat. Mika laughed and cried by turns. It was as if he'd never seen a living fish before. He didn't dare touch it himself, so I showed him how to break its neck. Then I put the mackerel into a fish pail.

"I'll ask Auntie Helen to cook it. We can eat it before we have our pancakes," I said.

"What are pancakes?" asked Mika.

I explained that Auntie Helen was going to make pancakes for lunch as a special treat and promised I'd try to smuggle out one or two for him.

I felt I just had to find out if Mika had been fishing before or if landing a mackerel on his first attempt was simply beginner's luck.

"Are there lots of fish in the sea on your planet?" I asked.

Mika shook his head. He looked as if he was going to cry.

"Well, I expect other animals live in it. Can you catch them?"

But again Mika shook his head.

"There used to be lots of plants and animals in the sea where I live, but the water got so polluted that everything in it died out," he said.

That sounded so sad and terrible that I felt almost like crying myself. So, to hide my feelings, I said that we had better row in again. When we reached the dock, I taught Mika how to tie up the boat.

So that was what our fishing trip was like. On the way back I carried the pail with the mackerel Mika had caught. He collected the magnifying glass from the flat rock, where he had left it.

All the way up to the house, Mika kept crouching down to examine everything he saw through the magnifying glass. He tried to inspect a greenfly that was scurrying about on a rosebush, but it wouldn't sit still. It obviously wasn't in the mood to be looked at.

"It's even smaller than a letter," he exclaimed. "Isn't it strange how something so tiny can be so alive?"

I didn't answer his question, but bowed deeply. I thought so too.

A little later we spotted a lizard crawling across a stone. Mika backed away.

"What was that?" he asked.

"A lizard," I said. "It's a reptile."

"So it's like a little dinosaur!" said Mika.

"That's right," I said. "There are much bigger reptiles, such as crocodiles, in some parts of the world, though none of them are as big as some of the dinosaurs were. But they all have scaly skin like dinosaurs, and they're all cold-blooded. Mind you, that doesn't mean they've got cold blood. It means that they can't control their body temperature. Their bodies are as warm or as cool as their surroundings. They have to bask in the sun to give themselves energy to move about."

His eyes widened.

"Can any of these reptiles talk?"

I laughed. "No, they're not advanced enough for that," I said. "Only humans can do that."

Just then, a cat came running down the

path toward us. I coaxed it over to me and bent down to stroke its silky coat. The cat meowed, then began to purr.

"I can't understand what it's saying," Mika complained.

"That's because cats can't talk," I told him.

"But I heard it say *meow, meow,* and then it made a noise like this," said Mika, trying to purr like the cat. "Isn't that talking? And if it can't talk, does that mean it can't think?"

I didn't know the answer to that. I was fairly sure that cats and cows couldn't think like us. I knew that many animals could learn certain skills, but a cat definitely didn't know it was a cat living on a planet that was orbiting a star in space.

"Is it a reptile?" Mika asked.

"No, and it's not an amphibian either," I said. "Cats are mammals."

"So they don't lay eggs," declared Mika.

He held the magnifying glass over the cat's nose.

"I think it must be good at smelling things," he said.

Then the cat ran off, and I began working out what to do with Mika when we got close to the house. Would I be able to keep him hidden from Auntie Helen?

I asked Mika if he'd like to wait in the shed. Lots of tiny animals lived in there, and he could look at them through the magnifying glass. When the coast was clear I'd come out to see him.

I went indoors clutching the fish pail. I hadn't given a thought to how I would explain the mackerel to Auntie Helen until she was standing right in front of me.

"What have you got there?" she asked, horrified, as if the fish was some dangerous monster.

"A fish," I said proudly.

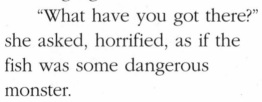

Can animals think?

"It's an animal that only lives in water. It's a vertebrate, which means it has a backbone. It doesn't have any lungs for breathing air like we do, so it breathes by taking in oxygen through feathery slits called gills. Even so, it's related to us, because we are descended from reptiles, reptiles are descended from amphibians, and amphibians are descended from the fish in the sea."

Auntie smiled and tousled my hair.

"I know you're a budding naturalist," she said. "But can you tell me where this particular fish came from?"

This was precisely the question I hadn't worked out an answer to yet. That was why I'd spouted all the other stuff.

"From someone who caught it," I said.

This was perfectly true. The odd thing was that Auntie didn't ask any more questions. She just took the pail with the fish in it and put it in the kitchen. Something told me she wasn't in the mood to gut a fish after all the trouble with the flour.

Dad phoned twice while we were having our pancakes. The baby still hadn't arrived, but Mom was all right and sent her love.

During the meal I went to the toilet twice,

which Auntie felt was a bit unnecessary. I managed to smuggle out half a pancake with me each time and hide it in a rubber boot in the hall.

"What would you like to do this afternoon, Joe?" Auntie Helen asked when we had finished. "Shall we go down to the sea?"

"No thank you," I said quickly. "I've got lots of things I want to do here."

"Fine," said Auntie Helen. "In that case I'll sit in the garden, and then I'm going to do some cooking so there's plenty of food in the house when your Mommy comes home with the baby."

While Auntie Helen was doing the dishes, I ran out to the shed to see Mika. There was no one there!

THE EGG

I sprinted around the house. Mika was sitting in the chicken run, a new-laid egg in his hands.

"Look, it's laid an egg!" he cried, as if that was something very special and mysterious.

We just kept the hens for fun, but they gave us enough eggs for our breakfast and for pancake days.

"Be careful," I warned him.

He nodded solemnly. "I will. Because a young animal might hatch from this egg."

"A chick," I said. "Birds developed from reptiles at some time, millions of years ago, just as mammals did."

Mika pointed at one of the hens.

"How often do they lay eggs?" he asked.

I bowed low for this question.

"Sometimes they lay eggs almost every day," I said. "No wild birds or reptiles can do that. Most of them usually only lay eggs once a year."

Mika looked so surprised that I couldn't help laughing.

"Human beings have kept hens for thousands of years and picked out the ones that laid the most eggs," I said. "In just the same way we've always kept the cows that gave most milk, the sheep that provide lots of wool, and the fastest, strongest horses. We call all these domestic animals."

Mika set the egg carefully down again and was soon outside the wire fence.

I could see Auntie Helen coming out into the garden with a deck chair, so we crept back to the house and into the kitchen. There Mika caught sight of some eggshells on a plate left over from Auntie Helen's pan-cake-making. The sight of them upset him so much that he clapped his hands over his eyes.

Despite this, he was soon seated at the kitchen table eating pancakes. He smeared so much jam over himself that he ended up in a disgusting state. When he'd finished eating, I led him to the bathroom.

I placed a stool by the bath and pushed Mika up onto the baby's new changing mat. I got my washcloth and started washing his face and tummy.

That was when I noticed! That's why I haven't told you until now: Mika had no navel! Do you see, Camilla? Can you imagine how startled I was?

All humans have a belly button in the middle of their tummies because once, when they were inside their mothers, they were fed through a tube joined to their navels called an umbilical cord. But Mika had no navel. So how had he been born?

I didn't know what to think. I just dried him with a towel and helped him down again. He ran into the little room above the hallway. My baby brother's room. Mika pointed to the cradle the baby was to sleep in and clambered up into it. I began to rock him gently back and forth so that he could see what a cradle was for. Mika laughed delightedly.

"This is for my baby brother when he's born," I explained. "This cradle is where he'll sleep."

"That's fine by me," retorted Mika, climbing out of the cradle. He looked a bit upset. "And I must get home before I start to wake up."

He looked about the room in a puzzled way. Then he said:

"I can't see any egg."

At that moment something began to dawn on me. You're getting warm, Camilla!

We went downstairs to the living room. On the shelf beneath the coffee table was a big photo album. I put it on the table and sat on the sofa. Mika sat down next to me.

"This is a photo album," I said.

He gazed up at me. I could see he hadn't

the faintest idea what a photo album was.

"Hang on a minute," I said.

I rushed up to my room and fetched my camera. I can even remember checking to see that the flash was working. Then I ran down again and took a picture of Mika. I made sure I had the whole of his tummy in the picture so that it would be quite obvious to everyone that he didn't have a navel.

Click! it went. I'll never forget that click. If Mika were suddenly to run off, at least now I'd have proof that I'd actually met him.

Mika was scared by the flash, and I had to put a comforting finger on his neck so he would not start crying. Then I opened the photo album.

"This book is full of pictures my family has taken of each other," I explained. "Now I'll be able to put a picture of you in here, too."

I pointed out all the pictures of Mom and Dad before they were married. Then we got to a photo of Mom with a big tummy, when I was just about to be born.

"That's me inside her tummy," I told him. "It's just before I came out."

It was clear that Mika had realized something.

"Live young," he murmured.

I flipped through the pages and found the picture Dad had taken of Mom and me when I was sucking milk from her breast.

"And this is me," I said. "When I was hungry, I got milk from Mom."

"Milk?" echoed Mika, wide-eyed.

I had to laugh. If Mika didn't understand what a mammal was, then of course he wouldn't know what milk was, either.

"It's food for little babies," I said.

He turned away from the photo album. I think he found looking at me sucking Mom's breast rather yucky.

"So how come we're both so alike, if you're a mammal and I'm not?" he asked.

I had been wondering the same thing. It was as if Mika had taken the words out of my mouth, so I didn't even bother to bow for the question he'd asked.

I should have thought of this before. Mika had come all the way from another planet in space, a planet with a totally different history from the earth's. So how was it we looked so alike?

It was a riddle that Mika eventually solved, Camilla. And soon I'll unravel it for you, too.

Just then I heard Auntie Helen coming in.

"Joe? Where are you? Are you all right? Why don't you go and play in the garden?"

I put my head around the living room door.

She was standing in the hall.

"I'm going out now," I said.

"Good. I'm going to start cooking," said Auntie.

She went into the kitchen. I took Mika's hand, and we tiptoed out through the front door and into the garden.

We climbed the high knoll in front of the house and sat down on a big pile of stones that Dad and I had once made. Mom and Dad had always called this little hill the Hummock. From there we could look down on the house and far out across the rocky coast and the sea.

The seagulls screeched
and wailed, which was fine
because they would drown
out Mika if he started to
do the same thing.

When we were sitting
on the Stone Seat down by
the cove, I'd told Mika about
the sea and how life on earth began. Now it
was his turn to tell me about life on the planet
he came from.

He still sucked his thumb occasionally and
fanned out his fingers, but when he began to
tell me about life on his planet, he sounded
a lot like Dad.

"The planet I come from is called Eljo," said
Mika. "And there, too, life began in the sea
several thousand million years ago. No one
knows how it happened. But now there are
many different kinds of animals on Eljo."

Just like here, I thought. Even though Mika
and I came from different planets, we were
really talking about the same thing.

He went on: "Hundreds of millions of years
ago some animals called mumbos developed on
Eljo. They laid eggs with hard shells. We have
no animals that give birth to live young."

"Where do people like you come from, then?" I burst out.

Mika was so excited that he didn't even stop to bow for my question. He sat splaying his fingers as he answered:

"On our planet, nothing has ever happened to make the mumbos die out. So for millions and millions of years they were able to evolve, slowly changing over time. Today a few mumbos can speak to one another and even ask questions about outer space. I am one of these mumbos myself."

I am one of these mumbos myself, Camilla!

"When I was about to come into the world," Mika went on, "I lay inside an egg that my mother and father placed on a cushion in a warm room. They never dared leave the egg alone. On Eljo, you see, we have some nasty animals that live by stealing the eggs of others. So they used to put the egg into a little stroller and push me around with them. They called the egg their treasure. On Eljo an egg is considered the most valuable treasure there is."

Now I was beginning to understand how Mika had been born.

"My arms and legs were soon so strong that the egg began to crack each time I kicked or

waved my arms about," said Mika. "While this was going on, my whole family sat around the cushion watching."

"And then . . . you just crawled out?" I cried.

Mika nodded.

"I can't remember anything about it at all, but I must have been dazzled by the bright light. Inside the egg it was almost completely dark, and very quiet. I suppose I just lay there sucking my fingers."

Are you listening carefully, Camilla? I found what Mika was saying thrilling and mysterious. But actually, it was no more mysterious than what I'd already told him about the earth's history and my baby brother who was soon to be born. Only then did I see why Mika had found it so difficult to understand what being a mammal was like.

The strangest thing of all had to do with us two. With such different backgrounds, how could we end up so alike?

Why are we so alike?

THE
MOUNTAIN

I still think it's likely that there really is life on other planets. I wonder if the rules about how life develops from single cells to thinking beings like you and me would be the same right across the universe? If so, life on these planets too must have evolved from tiny plants and animals as their environment changed.

Some people think that the dinosaurs died out because an asteroid struck the earth. When it happened, it was a matter of pure chance, like winning the lottery. But if that hadn't happened, dinosaurs would certainly have continued to evolve. Maybe it would have been their descendants who built cities and spacecraft, hospitals and computers, universities and gyms.

When the asteroid exploded, it showered

the sky with millions of tons of rock and dust, which blocked out the sun's heat. Many plants and animals, including the dinosaurs, died as the temperature dropped below freezing. Only animals that could survive the cold were left. So it was that humans became the first to set foot on the moon. They had evolved from the mammals that survived. The reptiles had lost the race.

"The good thing about visiting a strange planet is that it makes you understand your own planet a little better," Mika said. "You can see that every planet has its advantages and its disadvantages."

Now he sounded just like Dad—only Dad didn't wave his fingers or suck his thumb while he was talking.

"If you live in the mountains, you need to be a good climber," Mika went on. "On flat ground, it's more useful to be good at running. If you live near animals that might eat you, it's a good idea to taste disgusting or, even better, to be poisonous. But the best thing of all is to be clever."

I nodded vigorously. Then he said:

"Perhaps it's the same on every planet."

"What do you mean?" I asked.

He bowed solemnly.

"We're rather alike, don't you think?"

"Of course," I assured him. "But why?"

"Because we were both born to have children and grandchildren, so that mumbos and humans don't die out," he explained. "So we need to be able to do some of the same things."

"What things?" I asked.

"Well, we both need food to live and grow up healthy so that one day we can lay an egg or give birth to a baby. But not all food is fit for us to eat, so we need to taste it first. That's why we've both got tongues."

He stuck out his own tongue and then exclaimed:

"See, that's one way we're alike."

That's one way we're alike, Camilla! What do you imagine eating pancakes and strawberry jam would be like if you couldn't taste what you were eating? Or rotten eggs, for

that matter? Have you ever
tried counting how many
different things you can
taste?

Mika had put his thumb
in his mouth. Now he pulled it
out and started talking again.

"Mind you, by the time we realize something
tastes bad, it might already be poisoning us.
That's why it's useful to be able to smell things
before you taste them. It could even save your
life."

"We've both got noses, too," I
said. "We can smell our food
even before we taste it. There
are lots of animals that can sniff
out a tasty morsel, or smell an
enemy approaching, from a long way off. Smell
can even save your life."

It was a big mystery, how we could smell
things from a long way off. Some days before, I'd
been standing right down by the currant bushes
when my nose had told me that
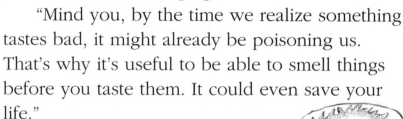
Mom had scones in the oven.
I'd run up to the house and
darted into the kitchen.
"Scones!" I'd shouted.

But how had the smell of those scones managed to travel through the air all the way to my nose by the currant bushes? How had my nose managed to tell my brain that it was smelling newly baked scones and not, for example, bread or buns?

"Do you like scones?" I asked.

"Scones?" Mika obviously hadn't a clue what they were. He went on:

"We may not like the same things, we may not even smell things the same, but being able to smell and taste matters just as much to me as it does to you."

Mika sat for a while toying with the heather that grew between the stones. He must have liked the way it tickled his fingertips.

"We can find out things by touch, too, can't we?" I said.

"Yes," said Mika, "because we're both covered in skin with tiny nerve endings all over it. When we touch something so hot it might burn us, or so sharp it might cut us, the nerves flash a signal to the brain. Quick as a wink the brain sends a message back telling us to get out of the way fast."

He jerked his hands back from the heather, just to show how quickly his brain could send a message to them. He pointed to the little cut on his finger.

"If I hadn't had nerves in my fingers, that fishhook would have hurt me much more than it did," he said.

"We both need to feel our surroundings!" I said quickly, before he got the chance to.

Mika nodded solemnly. The next moment he was looking up at me with a sly smile.

"And we both think it feels nice to have our necks stroked," he said.

He pointed up at some gulls that were wheeling overhead.

"Why do you think they're squealing like that?" he asked.

"Maybe they're telling one another where to find food."

He nodded.

"It must be a great advantage on both our planets to be able to hear things. For example, if danger threatens, it can be very useful to hear it a long way off so that we have time to hide, or even shout a warning to a younger sister or brother who is doing something stupid. But for this we need ears to hear with."

"We've got two ears," I said. "Couldn't we have managed with just one?"

Mika shook his head.

"If we only had one ear, we wouldn't be able to pinpoint where a sound was coming from. That's very important, so we can decide which way to run."

I glanced at Mika's ears. They were a little different from my own, but not much. Mika's ears were two small holes in his head, just like mine.

"That's another way we're alike," I said.

For a moment we sat quite still listening to the seagulls. Only occasionally was it quiet enough to hear the waves beating against the rocks.

"We can both hear the waves in the sea too," I said.

A few small sea pinks grew among the stones and heather. Mika picked one and held it up to his eyes.

"The really surprising thing is that we can see the world around us," he said.

"That's why we've got eyes to see with," I put in. "And we're like each other in that way too!"

The sun was quite low in the sky now. Mika pointed to its glowing face, just as he'd done when it had risen all those hours before.

"We can see where to find food, or spot danger approaching," he said. "But luckily, we can see more than just that. We can look each other in the eye and ask what the other person is thinking about. Or we can gaze into space and dream of life on other planets."

I sat pondering what Mika had said. Wasn't it strange that I could sit up on the Hummock and look across the sea simply because I'd been given a pair of eyes to see with?

Mika was silent for a long time, too, before he spoke again.

"An egg is a miracle . . ."

He'd said that earlier, but now he went on.

"Inside the egg a pair of eyes is forming,

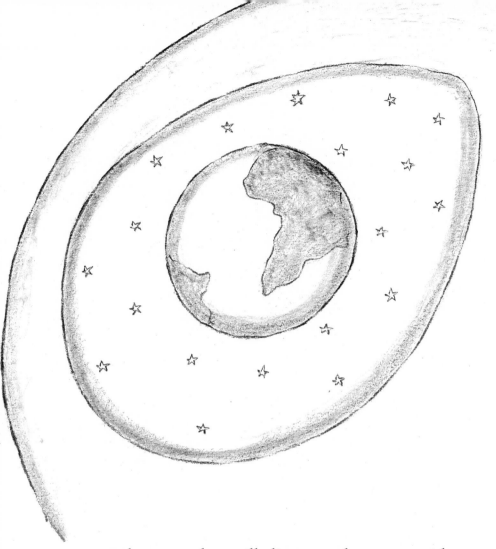

eyes that one day will discover the great wide world we're each a tiny part of. It's almost as if the whole world is growing inside that dark egg."

Or inside Mom's tummy, I thought. But I didn't say it out loud.

"There are all sorts of ways that we're alike," said Mika. "Both of us can taste, smell, feel, hear, and see things."

"But lots of other animals can do those things too," I put in. "And they don't look like us."

"Well, you and I don't need four legs to walk on," said Mika. "At some point, millions of years ago, both your ancestors and mine stood up on two legs, and their forelegs began to develop into arms and hands."

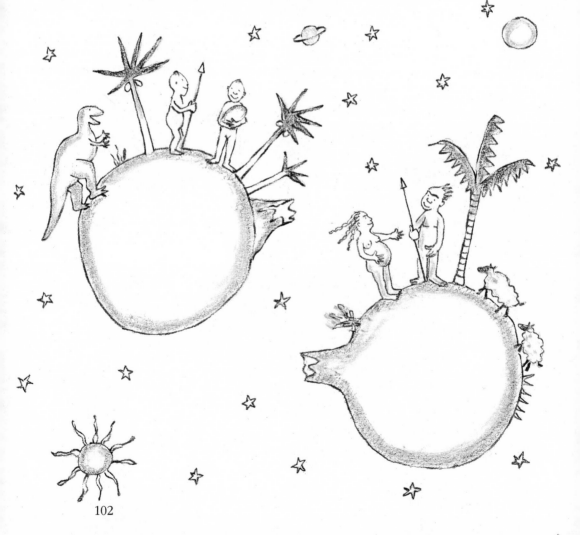

"That's right," I said. "Our ancestors were
ape-men who lived in forests. They needed
hands for gripping branches and plucking
leaves and fruit. They learned to use their hands
for throwing stones to defend themselves
against fierce animals. And, of course, they
began using their hands for making things."

This was something Dad and I had talked about. Dad had pointed out that when animals walked on all fours they couldn't do anything with their forelegs.

"But why don't we have four legs and two arms?" I asked. "Or three legs and six arms?"

These questions made Mika bow elegantly.

"Because the animals we are descended from only had four legs," he replied.

I'd often thought about this. Amphibians only had four legs. Just enough for two legs and two arms.

But even so, I wasn't completely satisfied with Mika's answer. Wasn't it odd that both he and I were descended from small creatures with four legs? Why couldn't one of us have come from an animal with six or eight legs?

It was as if he'd read my thoughts.

"I don't expect we'd be able to do all that much more with four hands instead of two," he said. "We don't need more than two legs to walk on, either. Enough is enough. There's no point in feeding more arms and legs than necessary."

Are you following this, Camilla? To this day, I find it extraordinary that amphibians really had all that was necessary to make a human being when they crawled out of the sea on four legs. No more and no less. It sometimes makes me wonder if they knew where they were going . . .

"So both mumbos and mammals raised themselves up on two legs," said Mika. "And their free hands were important in getting the brain to develop."

"Why?"

He bowed.

"Our ancestors could use their hands to make tools that made life easier for them. But for their hands to be of use, their brains had to develop, too. The ones who managed to do something clever with their hands had a big advantage over the ones that just let them dangle idly by their sides."

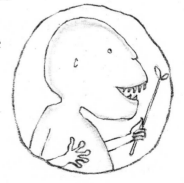

"Now we're starting to look more and more alike," I said.

He nodded. "Yes, we can both think."

"That's why we have such large heads," I said.

He didn't reply. But after a little while he looked up at me and asked something he must have been wondering about.

"Won't it hurt your mother a bit when your baby brother forces his head out of her body?"

"Yes," I said, biting my lip. I didn't like to think about that.

"Every planet has its disadvantages," said Mika.

"But there are people at the hospital to help her," I added quickly.

"Exactly!" he exclaimed, stretching and splaying his fingers. "Just what I was about to say."

"What was?"

"It's important for people like you and me to be able to help one another. So it's good that we can talk to each other. No one would be able to travel to another planet if he couldn't do that. That's another way we're alike."

I had been thinking much the same thing.

That's one small step for a man, one giant leap for mankind, the astronaut Neil Armstrong

had said as he placed his foot on the surface of the moon. When he said this, it was almost as if he'd taken the whole of mankind to the moon. He hadn't just traveled there for himself.

"That's one small step for a man, one giant leap for mankind," Mika murmured.

I started. "How did you know that was what I was thinking?" I asked.

Mika clapped one hand over his mouth. His cheeks turned red.

"Sorry!" he said.

I wanted to get to the bottom of this. How had Mika managed to say something I'd been thinking to myself? I'd never mentioned the moon landing in Mika's presence. Surely he hadn't been on the moon when Neil Armstrong had said those famous words?

"Sorry about what?"

"I said what you were thinking," he admitted. "It was a bit sneaky of me, but your thoughts seemed so interesting that I forgot myself."

He said it was common for the mumbos on Eljo to be able to read one another's thoughts. They could sometimes hold long conversations without exchanging a single word.

"It's very useful," he said. "I've only been on this planet for a few hours. How do you imagine I'd have been able to speak your language if I couldn't read your thoughts? And how do you think I could have learned so much about life on this planet?"

"We're not like you in that way," I said. "We can't read other people's thoughts."

"Well, perhaps you can do something else, something that mumbos can't do," Mika said kindly.

I tried to think of something clever we

could do. Then I remembered how frightened Mika had been when the phone rang.

"We have telephones, so we can speak to people who live on the other side of the earth," I said. "This whole planet is a tangle of telephone wires that we can talk through."

"Every planet has its advantages," Mika said enviously.

Are you paying attention, Camilla? I was really alarmed to find suddenly that Mika could read my

thoughts. But then, I think he was just as alarmed when I told him about the telephone. Today I might have told him about computers, too. We hardly need to be able to read one another's thoughts now that we have tele-phones, computers, and the Internet.

So I'd finally got some kind of explanation for how Mika could speak my own language and for how easily we could talk about life on earth. It was all because he'd been borrowing from my thoughts.

But it still seemed strange that we were so alike.

It was then, Camilla, that Mika told me about the mountain. He looked out across the landscape, then placed one hand solemnly on the pile of stones that Dad and I had built up.

"If you lived in one valley and I lived in another, couldn't we climb up out of our valleys and one day hold hands on top of a mountain?"

It was a question, so I quickly bowed for it, but I couldn't grasp what he meant. He went on:

"There might be lots of different ways of getting to the top of the mountain, but the mountain itself would stay exactly the same. And we must have been fairly alike to begin with, because each of us is a kind of mountain climber. There, at the top of that mountain, we might make a big pile of stones together. Then we might sit down and rest after the long climb. For once we might forget all our worries, large and small. We would have left them behind in the valleys."

"You mean that even though you come from one planet and I come from another we can still meet on the same mountain?" I asked.

He nodded.

Where are we going?

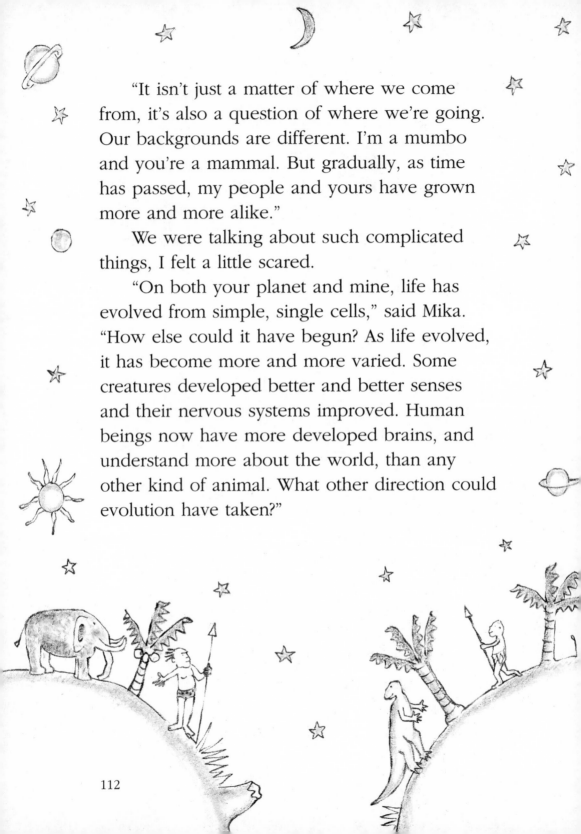

"It isn't just a matter of where we come from, it's also a question of where we're going. Our backgrounds are different. I'm a mumbo and you're a mammal. But gradually, as time has passed, my people and yours have grown more and more alike."

We were talking about such complicated things, I felt a little scared.

"On both your planet and mine, life has evolved from simple, single cells," said Mika. "How else could it have begun? As life evolved, it has become more and more varied. Some creatures developed better and better senses and their nervous systems improved. Human beings now have more developed brains, and understand more about the world, than any other kind of animal. What other direction could evolution have taken?"

I bowed for the question. I had no idea what the answer was.

"It all began in the deep oceans, which is all there was in the beginning," he said. "And now we're sitting here looking out over the rocky coast and the sea."

"Maybe that's what it was all for?"

Mika gazed out to sea.

"Once this planet lay sleeping," he said. "Then slowly it stirred to life. The sea splashed, the grass rustled, and wings flickered over the water. But only now is it awake, or almost awake. You who live here have gradually learned something of the history of your planet. You have been to the moon and discovered that magic point where down becomes up and up becomes down. And more than that: you have turned your gaze to the universe. Out there, perhaps, you have glimpsed a greater whole."

"Yes," I whispered, awestruck. "We have."

I didn't quite know what to say, because we'd almost reached the top of that mountain. Now it was the very mountain itself we were talking about and not just the long climb up it.

"Perhaps there are senses we still haven't got," I said at last.

"Yes, perhaps there are," said Mika. "We're sitting on a planet in space and talking about how it might all fit together. I would like to have a sense that would let me smell or see exactly where everything came from."

I didn't bow for this answer, but I took his wise words to heart.

A moment later he picked up a stone from the ground at our feet.

"What's this?" he asked.

"Just an ordinary piece of granite," I replied.

I thought it a very simple question, but Mika snorted scornfully.

"Nothing in the world is ordinary. Everything that exists is part of a great riddle. You and I are, too. We are the riddle no one can guess." He held up the stone so that I could see it better.

"Where does this stone come from? It's a

small piece of a planet, of course. And the planet is a small piece of the universe. But what is the universe? Where does the world come from?"

I had no answer to his question. I wouldn't even hazard a guess at the greatest riddle of them all.

Mika placed the stone at the very top of the pile. Now he's helped to build it too, I thought.

"Do you believe everything has come into being by itself?" I asked. "Or do you believe there's a God who has created it all?"

"I don't know," he said, "but I'm sure the dinosaurs and the ancient mumbos of Eljo never asked questions like that."

I laughed. "But we do," I said. "Asking difficult questions is something else we both do."

"Maybe asking questions, particularly questions without answers, is the most important of all our similarities," said Mika with a big grin.

Then he asked two questions that I've never forgotten.

Where does the world come from?

"If there is a God, who is he? And if there isn't a God, what is the universe?"

It took me a long time to think these questions over. If there was a God who had created the entire universe, who was he? And what was he? And where was he? And if a God hadn't created the universe, what is it and where has it come from? Where is its center and where does it end?

"What do you believe?" I asked him again.

Mika made a deep bow.

"I'm not so sure that the universe is an accident."

"But do you believe in a God who made it all?"

Again he bowed.

"Will you promise to take an answer for an answer?" he asked.

"Of course," I said. I thought that he meant I should treat his answer merely as an answer. By which he meant that an answer was worth much less than a question.

His eyes seemed to flash.

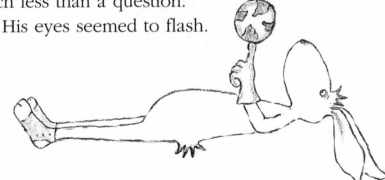

"The force of gravity makes your planet orbit the sun, and the force of gravity from the moon pulls at the sea and makes tides rise and fall. Don't you think there must also be a force that dragged you up from the oceans and gave you eyes for seeing and a brain for thinking?"

I didn't know what to say.

"I sometimes wonder if people who don't believe this are missing an important sense," said Mika finally.

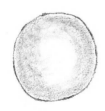

7

THE
NIGHT

The sun was just about to dip beneath the rocks. Suddenly we heard a sharp call rising above the din of the seagulls.

"Joe! Where are you?"

It was Auntie Helen. She was searching for me in the garden below. She might look up at the Hummock at any moment—she knew I sometimes went up there to sit and ponder things.

"I'll have to go indoors," I said. "It must be nearly my bedtime."

I jumped to my feet and dashed off. As I ran I heard Mika's voice behind me.

"Maybe I'll wake up soon, now."

I met Auntie on the garden path. Dad had phoned again and said the baby still hadn't arrived. Now I must have my supper and go to bed.

While I ate, I thought about Mika. I had just run off and left him. Where was he now? Would he be able to take care of himself? And what had he meant when he said he might soon wake up?

Shortly afterward, I was in bed ready to go to sleep. Auntie Helen had said good night and switched off the light. She was going to sleep downstairs on the sofa. The last thing she said before she went out was:

"Just think, Joe, by the time you wake up your little sister or brother will have arrived."

Then I began to think about my baby brother.

Well, at least I'd had some good practice at talking about the world. I was the one who would have to tell him how everything here had come into existence.

I think I must have slept for a while. Suddenly I was woken by a tapping on my window. It was Mika! He'd managed to climb onto the roof. I got out of bed and opened the window.

"Ssh!" I said.

"Do you want to come out and look at the stars with me?" he whispered.

I was worried that my aunt might suddenly

come up to my room, but I pulled on my
clothes and slippers again, clambered out of the
window, and went up onto the roof with Mika.
We climbed right up to the ridge. The air was
rather chilly, so we huddled close together.

It was another brilliant starlit night.

Mika pointed up to a particular star shining extra brightly.

"Perhaps that's my sun we can see up there," he said solemnly.

"Or down there," I put in. "After all, you journeyed upward until you banged your head on this planet."

I couldn't stop thinking that Mika had once hatched out of an egg.

"How long ago did you crawl out of your egg on Eljo, Mika?" I asked him.

He bowed for the question.

"Precisely one year ago."

"Happy birthday!" I exclaimed. "But I was born eight years ago, so I'm older than you."

"A year on Eljo is a lot longer

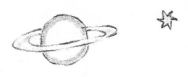

than a year here," said Mika. "It's a question of how quickly a planet goes around its sun."

"The earth takes 365 and a quarter days to go around the sun," I said. "So we have to add an extra day every four years to even it out." I knew that a year can be much shorter or longer on another planet.

"Our days are longer than yours, too," Mika said. "It only seems a short time ago that the sun rose on a new day. And now it's night again already."

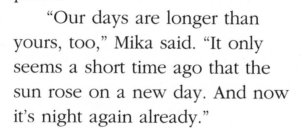

"A day is twenty-four hours, because the earth takes twenty-four hours to spin around once," I explained.

"What are hours?" asked Mika.

Suddenly I realized that the idea of twenty-four hours was just something we had invented here

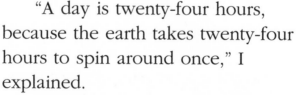

125

on our own planet. We could just as easily have made each day ten hours long with, perhaps, a hundred minutes to every hour.

"We've divided the day into twenty-four hours," I said. "And there are sixty minutes in each hour. Then each minute is divided into sixty seconds."

"I see," said Mika, who was listening carefully. "And how long is a second?"

"One! . . . two! . . . three!" I went. "That was roughly a second between each number."

Mika sat thinking and stretching his fingers. I realized he was working something out. At last he said:

"In that case you'd be one year and eight days old on my planet."

So I was eight days older than Mika. I found that last sum the easiest.

The stars shone like needles in the night sky.

"Why did you come here?" I asked Mika.

"To meet you. You don't really believe that I happened to fall into your garden by accident just when you were home alone and waiting for a baby brother?"

I thought this a good question, so I bowed

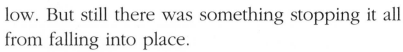

low. But still there was something stopping it all
from falling into place.

"But it's all just a dream," said Mika.

"What is?"

He sat waving his fingers as he replied:

"I dreamed I flew out into space with my
spaceship. For a long time all I saw were stars
and galaxies. Now and again I caught a glimpse
of a comet. But then one day I entered a solar
system. First I flew past a small, cold planet
right on the edge of the solar system. Then I
went by some big planets with moons and
broad rings around them. That was when I
suddenly spotted a little
blue-green pearl in
the distance. It
looked a bit like
a jawbreaker. I
wondered if it
had life on it."

"It was the
earth," I said.
"And it isn't a
dream."

He shook
his head.

"Oh no, but I dreamed I could see it. I was so curious I opened a hatch in the spaceship. 'Hello?' I shouted out into the night. 'Is anybody there? Or is it all empty and deserted?'"

I tried to picture the scene.

"The next moment I had tumbled through the hatch and was hurtling toward the strange planet's surface at an enormous speed. 'Help!' I shouted—even though I knew no one was there to help me. 'I'm falling!'"

"You must have been really frightened!" I exclaimed.

He nodded.

"But soon I was dangling in an apple tree just above the ground. And you know the rest of the story."

He was right there. I had seen it all with my own eyes.

"I knew it was a dream all the time," said Mika, "but the dream just went on and on."

"Perhaps you dreamed that you hatched out of an egg, too," I put in.

He shook his head.

"I'm as sure of it as I am that we're both sitting up here on the roof together gazing into space."

"But if your journey to this planet was just a

dream, then the fact we're sitting together on the roof must also be a dream. And if so, one of us must be dreaming."

Mika nodded. "All planets have two sides, and both sides can't face the sun at once. It's usually the same with our dreams. The person who dreams and the person who is dreamed of aren't always awake or asleep at the same time."

"In that case I wonder if it's you or me who's dreaming," I said.

"It doesn't make any difference," he said, brushing it aside. "The most important thing is that we met each other on the top of that mountain. People don't go up there very often."

"But if I'm the one dreaming about you," I said, "you couldn't have existed before I started dreaming. And you'll vanish, too, the moment I wake up."

"How can you be so sure you're the only person who dreams about me?" asked Mika. "And how can you be so sure you won't dream about me again?"

His questions struck me like a thunderbolt. All I could do was shake my head. I didn't even try to answer. What Mika had said seemed to give a whole new meaning to everything we'd been talking about.

It was only then that I realized I was shivering with cold. I had begun to yawn too. But I didn't want to be parted from Mika.

"I've got a plan," I said.

"You've got a whole planet," said Mika. He had an odd, blank expression on his face.

"I mean I've got a good idea," I explained. Now *my* fingers were beginning to wave.

"Lucky you."

I was worried in case he'd already begun to wake up. If he had, mightn't he just disappear right in front of my eyes?

I hurried to share my idea with him.

"You can sleep under my bed for the night," I said.

I think he was glad of my offer. Kindness and consideration must be popular in every corner of the universe. But there was also something sad in his voice as he replied:

"Well, at least I can come to your room with you."

We crept quickly back through the window and down onto the floor inside.

"It must be nice living in such a lovely house," he said.

He looked around the room as if for the first and last time. Then he added:

"I'm sure it'll be fun to have a baby brother, too."

At the foot of my bed was a blanket to put over my comforter when it was cold. I spread the blanket on the floor under my bed.

"You can sleep here," I said. "But you must promise to keep as quiet as a mouse when my aunt comes."

He had begun to spin my globe. He twirled it around and around, faster and faster.

"I won't make a sound," he said.

"Do you know it's more than twelve hours since we met," I said.

"Or just a few minutes," he replied.

"It seems hours and hours to me, at any rate," I said. "When we wake up early tomor-row it will have been a full day."

He stabbed at the globe with one of his fingers so that it stopped abruptly. He looked up at me and said eagerly:

"Traveling brings you farther out into the world. Dreaming draws you farther inside it. But maybe we can't travel in more than one direction at once."

I've always remembered these words. I never cease to wonder at outer space. But I also never stop marveling that I have a head and a mind that take me into my very own personal world.

Mika crawled under the bed and lay down on the blanket.

"Good night," I said.

"Or good morning," he replied. "Don't forget, the earth is spinning around and around."

I laid my head on the pillow. Suddenly I heard a voice whispering into my ear.

"It has taken thousands of millions of years to create beings like us, who can think and dream, remember and forget," said the voice. "A whole world awaits us."

Those were the last words Mika ever spoke to me. He must have crawled back under the bed again. Soon we were both fast asleep.

THE HAT

A little later I was awakened by my aunt coming into the room. The first thing that went through my mind was that the night had passed very quickly.

Auntie Helen came up to the bed and leaned over me. I was terrified that Mika would pinch her leg.

"Wake up, Joe," she said, beaming.

I wasn't quite awake yet, and I had to rub the sleep out of my eyes. Auntie Helen sat down on the edge of the bed and ruffled my hair.

"Wake up, Joe!" she said again. "You've got a little brother. Dad called from the hospital."

What is a friend?

At that I was wide-awake. My baby brother had arrived in the world!

"I knew it would be a boy," I said.

Auntie Helen said she was going to boil some eggs for breakfast. Dad would be home soon, and he would take me to the hospital to see the baby.

As soon as Auntie had gone I bent down and peered beneath the bed.

"Ssh!" I said.

But there was no one there. It was only then that I noticed Mika's blanket lying on the floor by the bed.

Two thoughts rushed through my mind at once. Mika had woken up, that was why he wasn't under the bed. But had he managed to get home to Eljo before he was fully awake? And if he hadn't gotten home, where would he be?

Something else was missing, too—my white rabbit. Before I met Mika the rabbit was my only real friend. Now it was nowhere to be seen.

If Mika had taken it with him because he felt the journey through space on his own might be a bit lonely, that was fine by me. After all, I'd gotten a baby brother.

After I'd been to the bathroom, I went

down to the kitchen, where
Auntie Helen was setting the
table for breakfast. I had to
think long and hard before
asking her to cut off the
head of my egg for me. That
was what we always used to
call it in my family.

　　After breakfast I was upstairs playing with
my Lego when I heard the car. Auntie Helen
and I both rushed to the front door. Dad was
standing on the doorstep ringing the bell—he'd
forgotten his key. For a moment I thought of
Mika and how terrified the ringing would make
him, but then I remembered
he was probably heading
out of the solar system
at top speed.

　　Dad gave me a
great big hug and
lifted me high into
the air.

"You've got a wonderful little brother, Joe!" he said. "I'm going to change my shirt and brush my teeth, then you can come along to the hospital and meet him and see Mommy."

After everything that had happened, I began to cry. Dad was almost crying, too. I've never understood why I cried then, just when I was so happy that my baby brother had been born. I just blubbered and blubbered for ages, while Dad held me in his arms.

We gave Auntie Helen a lift into town, but she wasn't allowed to meet the baby. Only immediate family could see Mom and the baby that day.

It was my turn first. Mom reached out and hugged me, but I thought she didn't look very well. She was much paler than usual. My baby brother lay on a tiny bed in a large room with several other newly born earthlings.

I was a bit disappointed when I saw the baby for the first time. He was smaller and redder in the face than I'd imagined, and he was sleeping soundly.

But then something
happened. Little by
little he began to
wake up. First he
started flexing and
stretching his thin
fingers. Then he began
to suck his hand.

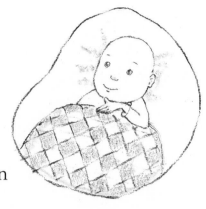

   He couldn't talk yet, and perhaps he
couldn't think, either. Even so it was obvious
that he was truly amazed by the world he'd
arrived in. It was as if he
were trying to grab at
something in the air
and was waving his
fingers because he
wanted to tell me
something.

   I remembered
the very last thing
Mika had said to me.
Now I spoke the same
words to my baby brother.
   "Happy birthday, brother," I
said. "A whole world awaits you!"
   A few days later Mom brought the baby
home from the hospital.

I'd drawn a pretty picture for him, showing the earth the way it looks from outer space. Here's the picture:

For the first few days and weeks the baby grabbed too much attention for my liking. Sometimes he'd scream so loudly I'd have to stick my fingers in my ears. When Mom was there, he usually quieted down pretty quickly. As soon as he got some milk from her, he would stop crying. It wasn't so easy for Dad or me to comfort him.

I was busy doing all sorts of things, but I remember that I kept looking for my white rabbit. I knew that maybe I didn't need it any longer, now that I'd gotten a real brother, but all the same, I was curious to know what had happened to it.

Sometimes I would search for Mika as well. I've carried on doing that all my life. Each time I sit on the Stone Seat down by the dock or up on the Hummock in front of the old pile of stones, I think about the long conversations I had with the mumbo from Eljo.

And then there's something else I've got to tell you, Camilla. I feel a bit embarrassed about it, but I must tell you all the same.

I said nothing to Mom and Dad about Mika, but I told Dad that I'd taken some funny pictures while Mom and he were at the hospital. I gave him my camera and asked him to get them developed for me. You can't imagine what a stupid thing I had done, Camilla: there was no film in the camera!

The baby was going to be called Michael.

Mom and Dad had thought the two names went well together—Joseph and Michael. I can't remember exactly when it was settled. Maybe I had a hand in choosing the name myself. But then again, perhaps Mom and Dad had made up their minds even before he was born.

But they couldn't have been sure it would be a boy, Camilla. That was something only I knew. Things are different today. Nowadays hospitals can use ultrasound to tell if the baby in the mother's tummy is a boy or a girl.

Now you're probably wondering if I really did meet Mika or if the whole thing was just a dream.

I bow right down to the ground for that, as I have often asked myself the same question.

When two people raise their heads out of their valleys and meet each other high up on the mountain, it hardly matters what the mountain is called, or where the two come from. When we stand on the top of a mountain, it feels as if we're on top of the world. And on the night my baby brother was born—well, I really was on top of the world.

I believe that some of the most important meetings in our lives take place while we are asleep. In the course of our lives, there are a few dreams that are so vivid they seem more real than life down in the valleys.

My encounter with Mika made me want to become an astronomer when I grew up, and that's what I did. My entire adult life has been spent studying outer space. Of course, I've taken time off to peer down into the odd stroller, but as far as I'm concerned that's rather like gazing up at the stars.

Sometimes, when I'm looking into space, it strikes me that what I'm really searching for up there is Mika.

Well, Camilla, this is the story I promised you. I decided when you were here on vacation that one day I would tell you about Mika, and since you'll be getting a baby brother or sister yourself, there couldn't be a better opportunity. Now you know what to expect!

I've tried to tell you everything just as I recall it. There are bits I must have forgotten, and bits I've probably imagined, but it's often like that when we try to describe things that happened long ago.

I believe that each night we forget a little of what we've seen and lived through. But at the same time, our minds are working really hard while we're sleeping. That's when we sink deep

Who am I?

into our own dreamworlds. It's as if we glide out of this world and into a totally new one. I find it strange to think about.

Perhaps we dream at night because our minds attempt to fill the hole left by all we forget while we're sleeping. And when we wake up in the morning, all we dreamed of soon disappears, like dew in the morning sunshine. I think we see and live through so many things during the day that our heads haven't got room for all of our dreams.

Remembering a dream is almost as hard as catching a bird in your hand, but sometimes it's as if the bird comes and sits on your shoulder of its own free will.

With love from

Uncle Joe